D1094680

JACK AND THE BEANSTALK

This is the story of a young boy named Jack, who lived in a tumble-down cottage with his mother.

They were so poor they had barely enough money for food. One day, Jack's mother found to her despair that they had no money left at all — not even one penny.

''There is only one thing left to do,'' sighed Jack's mother, ''we must sell our cow Buttercup, as she is the only thing we have left in the world.''

So Jack promised to go to market the following day to sell Buttercup for as much money as he could.

Early next morning before it was light, Jack left for market. He crept out of the house while his mother was still asleep. She was very fond of the cow, and would have found it hard to say goodbye.

Jack hadn't gone very far along the road before he met a pedlar.

"I will buy your cow in exchange for these five magic beans," the stranger said as he held out his hand. "Plant them and you will grow rich."

Young Jack couldn't resist. He gave Buttercup to the pedlar, grabbed the magic beans, and ran home to tell his mother.

She was rather surprised to see him back from market so soon. When she heard about the magic beans, she was so angry she tossed them out of the window. And poor silly Jack was sent to bed without any supper.

The next morning dawned dark and gloomy. Jack jumped out of bed and looked out of the window. The sky above was dark — not with clouds — but with giant green leaves! To Jack's amazement the magic beans had grown in the night. They were so tall, they covered the tiny cottage and disappeared up into the sky.

Jack had to push open the cottage door with all his might, he stepped outside and began to climb the beanstalk. The branches of the bean plant were so thick they formed a ladder, and soon Jack had climbed so high that his cottage was just a tiny speck down below.

At last the branches grew thinner and Jack knew he had reached the top. Ahead of him was a long road, which led to a mysterious castle in the distance. Bravely, Jack marched along until he reached the castle door. Loudly he knocked and waited.

It was opened by the most enormous woman Jack had ever seen. "Come in and eat," her great voice boomed. "Beware my husband the Giant — or he will eat you!"

Jack turned pale. "Don't be afraid," laughed the Giantess as she led Jack into her kitchen. The kind woman gave him a plate of food almost as high as himself. Jack had only taken two mouthfuls, when the whole room began to shake.

"My husband the Giant is home," cried the Giantess, and with that, she pushed Jack into the cupboard.

Not a moment too soon, for when the Giant strode into the room, he began to sniff around Jack's cupboard:

"Fee, fi, fo, fum,
I smell the blood of an Englishman;
Be he alive or be he dead,
I'll grind his bones to make my bread."

His wife smiled, "It's only the giant meat pie I cooked for your dinner that you can smell."

When he had gobbled up every scrap of food,
the Giant hammered on the table with his great fists.
"Wife," he called, "bring me my hen that lays golden eggs."

Jack could hardly believe his eyes when he
peeped out of the cupboard.

"Lay golden eggs," commanded the Giant.
And the little brown hen, which the Giant had placed
on the table, began to lay golden eggs. The Giant
scooped up the eggs, put them in his pocket and fell
fast asleep.

Jack saw his chance. He
jumped out of the cupboard,
snatched up the hen and ran for
his life until he reached the top
of the beanstalk.

He slid down the thick branches at top speed. His mother was overjoyed to see him back safe and sound. The little brown hen laid lots of eggs and made their fortune. Jack bought their cow Buttercup back and all three of them were very happy.

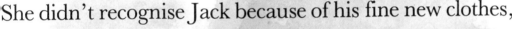

After a while, Jack longed to climb the beanstalk once more. So early one morning, before anyone could stop him, he climbed it again in search of adventure. Higher and higher he went, until he saw the winding road he knew led to the Giant's castle. Once again the castle door was opened by the Giant's wife. She didn't recognise Jack because of his fine new clothes, so she asked him in.

No sooner had Jack reached the kitchen, than the Giant returned. Jack looked around in panic.

''Hide in the log basket by the oven,'' begged the Giant's frightened wife.

Sure enough, the Giant strode straight over to where Jack was hiding.

''Fee, fi, fo, fum,

I smell the blood of an Englishman;

Be he alive or be he dead,

I'll grind his bones to make my bread.''

''It's only the soup I made for you this morning,'' said his wife, as she placed the huge bowl on the table in front of him.

What a noise the Giant made drinking his soup! As soon as he had finished, he took down a beautiful golden harp from the shelf above him. "Play me a lullaby," the Giant commanded the golden harp.

Jack had never heard such lovely music in his life. He knew he must have the harp for his very own. Such sweet music came from the harp, that the Giant soon fell into a deep sleep.

Jack saw his chance and seized the harp from the table. But as he ran out of the castle gates, the harp began to play loudly, "Help me, Master. Help me!"

The Giant awoke just in time to see Jack disappearing with his harp out of the castle gates. He thundered after the boy, screaming and roaring: "You stole my hen — you shall not have my golden harp!" And he chased Jack towards the beanstalk.

Jack slid down the branches in fear of his life. He could feel the beanstalk swaying and cracking as the Giant began to climb down after him. Now the Giant was as slow as Jack was nimble. So, when the boy reached the bottom of the beanstalk, he grabbed an axe and chopped at the branches with all his might.

The whole thing began to sway. With a few more blows of Jack's axe, the whole beanstalk came crashing down — bringing the Giant with it. His great weight made a huge hole in the ground, into which he vanished and was never seen again!

Jack and his mother lived happily ever after, together with the golden harp the little brown hen, and of course, their cow named Buttercup!

THE PRINCESS AND THE PEA

Once upon a time, there was a young Prince who decided to get married. ''You must marry a real, genuine Princess,'' insisted his mother the Queen. ''She must be beautiful, clever, charming and kind. Nothing less will do!'' And with that, she ordered the Prince's horse to be saddled and told him to ride off and start looking at once.

As there were no Princesses in his own kingdom, the Prince had to travel to every country in the world to look for one.

He met lots of them on his journey, but not one was perfect. Some were too tall and some were much too small, others too fat and some too thin. Some were very old and some were just babies.

The poor Prince was really disappointed. "I just can't seem to find a real, genuine Princess anywhere," he sighed. So, he climbed on his horse and began the long ride back to his kingdom. When, at last, he returned home, he decided to give up the idea altogether.

One dark night there was the most terrible storm. The wind howled and rain fell by the bucketful. Great flashes of lightning lit up the sky, and thunder shook the Palace walls.

In spite of all this noise, the King heard the tiniest knock on the Palace door.

"Now, who can be calling on a night like this?" snorted the Queen, for she was warm and comfortable and did not want to be disturbed. However, the kindly old King got up from his chair and went to open the door himself.

There standing in the doorway, was a young
girl. Her clothes were soaking and her shoes were
spattered with mud. Rainwater ran down her face and
her long golden hair was all wet and bedraggled. What
a sight she looked!

''I am a Princess. Please may I come in?'' she
whispered.

''Princess or not,'' said the King. ''Come in
by the fire and get warm,'' and he led her by the hand
into the great hall of his Palace.

When the Prince saw her standing in the
firelight, he fell in love with her and wanted to marry
her at once.

The Queen took one look at the girl dripping water on her best carpet and frowned. "She can't be a real, genuine Princess and look such a mess," she muttered to herself. "I've never heard such a tale in all my life!"

With that, she marched off towards the Palace kitchens. And there, from the store cupboard, she took one tiny dried pea. Then she crept quietly up the back stairs into the very best guest room.

"We'll soon see if she's a real, genuine Princess," and she placed the pea right in the centre of the Princess's bed.

Next, the Queen sent for all the maids in the Palace. "Bring me twenty mattresses from your linen cupboard at once."

The maids looked surprised, but were soon scurrying up and down the corridors puffing and panting under the weight of all those mattresses.

"Pile them up high on the bed!" yelled the Queen. "Now fetch me twenty of your softest feather quilts," the Queen ordered in her sternest voice. So the maids brought the feather quilts. By now everyone was quite out of breath.

"Now place the twenty feather quilts on top of the twenty mattresses," the Queen went on.

The pile of mattresses was so high that the maids could no longer reach them. So the Queen ordered her pageboys to bring long ladders. They pulled the twenty quilts up the ladders until, at last, the job was done and the Queen was satisfied.

While all this was going on the Princess had dried out from her soaking and was ready for bed.

She climbed up the ladder right to the top of the twenty mattresses and twenty feather quilts.

"Now we shall see if she is a real, genuine Princess," smiled the Queen.

Next morning, the storm had passed. The wind had died down and the storm clouds had gone from the sky. Bright sunshine streamed in through the Palace windows, and it was a beautiful day.

The Princess, however, came in to breakfast looking very pale and tired.

"Did you sleep well?" the Queen asked her.

"No, indeed I did not," she replied with a yawn. "In fact, I couldn't sleep a wink." And the poor Princess rubbed her back. "I think I must have been lying on a rock, the bed felt so hard and uncomfortable."

The Prince looked at the King in dismay —
but the Queen told them not to worry. How she
laughed as she led the Princess back to her bedroom.

One by one the pageboys took away the
feather quilts. Then one by one the maids took away
the mattresses. And there, lying right in the middle of
the bed, was one tiny dried PEA!

"Only a real, genuine Princess could feel a
tiny dried pea through all those quilts and
mattresses," laughed the Queen with delight.